Christmas Tree Farm

Sandra Jordan
CHRISTMAS TREE FARM

ORCHARD BOOKS
New York

For my dear sister Nan

ORCHARD BOOKS • 95 MADISON AVENUE • NEW YORK, NY 10016

Library of Congress Cataloging-in-Publication Data

Jordan, Sandra, date.
    Christmas tree farm / Sandra Jordan.
      p. cm.
    Summary: Describes the activities that take place on a Christmas tree farm in Rhode Island throughout each season of the year.
    ISBN 0-531-05499-3. — ISBN 0-531-08649-6 (lib. bdg.)
      1. Christmas tree growing—Juvenile literature.   2. Christmas tree growing—Rhode Island—Tiverton (Town)—Juvenile literature.
[1. Christmas trees. 2. Tree farms.] I. Title.
SB428.3.J67 1993
635.9'7752—dc20   93-20142

Manufactured in the United States of America

Printed by Barton Press, Inc.
Bound by Horowitz/Rae
BOOK DESIGN BY ANTLER & BALDWIN DESIGN GROUP

10 9 8 7 6 5 4 3 2 1

The text of this book is set in 14 point ITC Leawood Book.
The illustrations are hand-colored, sepia-toned photographs.

Down Main Road past Four Corners, near Nonquit Pond,
is Christmas Tree Farm.
When November days grow short and cold we go there,
racing through the fields on a hunt for the perfect tree.
Then we really know—Christmas is coming.

The farm belongs to
our friends Janice and Leo Clark.
Janice grew up there.
Her great-grandfather bought the land.
Her father built the house before she was born.
After Leo retired,
the Clarks moved back to the farm.
Now all year long they look after
their Christmas trees,
getting ready for this special season.

In early spring bags and cartons
of baby trees, raised by nurseries
from the seeds found in cones,
are delivered to the farm.

Leo and Janice do the planting,
helped by their children, their grandchildren,
and some young neighbors who live nearby.
The workers walk along the rows.
In the spaces between the trees
they look for stumps
from Christmas trees
cut down last year.
When they find one,
they plant a new seedling
next to it
in the damp spring earth.

There is always something to do
at the farm—seedlings to water,
weeds to pull, grass to cut.
By July the trees look
shaggy with their new growth
of long soft shoots.
The Clarks and their helpers
prune the trees
into a tidy Christmas tree shape.
Leo has a special saw that straps on.
With it a whole tree
can be trimmed at once.
He says he is giving the
tree a haircut.

In the fall,
about when the leaves change from green
to red and yellow,
the trees are measured
against one of Leo's long white sticks
and tied
with different colored tapes
so buyers can see how tall they are—
yellow, five feet;
blue, six feet;
red-and-white-striped, over seven feet.
It takes between ten and fifteen years
for a tree to grow
to red-and-white-striped size.

Some families want to plant
their trees after Christmas.
So gardeners come to the farm to
dig up sixty or seventy trees
and wrap the roots
into big
burlap-covered balls.

Then Leo and Janice decorate the field shack
where trees will be sold,
and stack firewood
beside the woodburning stove.
Everything is ready for Opening Day
of Christmas Tree Farm.

We come early on that November morning,
but we aren't the first ones there.
We see familiar faces.
Old friends and new stop by.
Some work on the farm;
some want to buy a tree;
others just want to say
hello and have a glass of Leo's apple cider.
It's like a neighborhood party.

The fields are full of people
picking out their trees.
When a tree is chosen, a field worker
puts a tag on the top.
Some families hang a few decorations
to celebrate their choice.
We made gold stars for our tree,
but we can't decide!
Do we want a tall skinny tree
or a small cozy one?
A long-needled white pine,
a short-needled spruce,
or a fir?
"Every tree is perfect in its own way,"
says Janice. "Every family likes
a different perfect tree. You will find
the right tree for you."

At last we all agree,
we have found *our* perfect tree.
We put our stars on it,
and they swing gently in the wind.
Mother says we can't take it home
till the week before Christmas.
Then we will come back
to cut it down.

Now we pay for it in the field shack.
The Clarks' daughter Pam
watches over
one of her sons who is cashier—
but he doesn't need any help.

In the middle of December
the cutting starts.
The red baler is busy
all day long.
A bushy tree goes in one end,
the men tug, and
out the tree comes—
made smaller by a net that holds
the branches close to the trunk.
That way it is easier to carry home.

On a frosty morning the week
before Christmas we cut our tree!
Joe, who is helping out,
goes to the field with us.
We take turns using his saw.
The pine needles are prickly.
The trunk is thick.
From under the tree
Joe says, "Give a push
so it falls in the right direction."
"There it goes!"
"Look out!"

We load it into the cart
and pile in too.
The tree smells spicy.
The long needles brush our chins.
We smile and smile.

All around us people
are taking home their trees.
"Good-bye," says Leo.
"See you next year."
"Merry Christmas," says Janice.
"Good-bye."

Our tree rises
to the ceiling—
full of bright ornaments
and mysterious shadows.
We hold hands and sing
of angels we have heard on high,
of hope for peace on earth,
and goodwill to everyone.

Christmas is over.
We go for a walk
on the farm.
The field shack stands silent,
empty until next year.
The trees glisten under the January snow.
They are resting,
waiting for spring.
We hear the snow
crunching under our boots,
and the songs of winter birds.

The snow melts.
Dandelions and violets
bloom in the grass.
Soon the spruces,
pines, and firs will have
long soft shoots of new growth.
And this spring, like every spring,
the Clarks plant new trees to grow
where last year's stood,
on Christmas Tree Farm.

What happens to Christmas trees when Christmas is over? In one tradition the trunk is cut into Yule logs, decorated, and ceremoniously burned in the fireplace as part of the next year's Christmas Eve celebration.

In Tiverton, Rhode Island, where the Clarks live, a truck collects the undecorated trees. Every ornament and strand of tinsel must be removed. The trees are put through a special machine that grinds them up and turns them into garden mulch. The mulch is left in a huge pile, and anyone who needs it is welcome to take away a bushel or a truckload. Another community nearby uses the old Christmas trees to keep the sand dunes in place when the winter winds blow hard off the ocean.

What happens to Christmas trees in your town?

Thank you to all of the Clark family of Clark's Tree Farm in Tiverton, Rhode Island—Leo and Janice; Pam Clark Thurlow, her husband Chip, and their twin boys Chris and Andrew; Polly Clark Ney, her husband Joe, their son Bill, and their daughter Margaret. Thank you to the many other terrific people who work at Clark's—Billy Sanford, Mike, Sean, and Tommy. And a special thank-you to my sister Nan, her husband Robert, his son Scot, and their children Katherine, Michael, and Max. Many thanks also to my old friends and new who helped me out when I needed it—Ann Beneduce; Lance Newman; John Foley and Lisa, Jane, and Daniel Finn-Foley; Diana, Sheldon, Mia, and Simon Lidofsky; Bronwyn Roberts; Jonathon Hutton; Kathryn and Jessica Bondi; and Nancy Arnold.